Anna and the Bagpiper

Anna and the Bagpiper

THOMAS LOCKER

PHILOMEL BOOKS

Early one evening Anna was listening to the birds sing
when suddenly the world became almost silent.

Anna thought she heard a strange, faraway sound coming from the hilltop. It seemed to call her.

Standing on her tiptoes, Anna discovered she could reach the gate latch.

The sound grew louder and louder as she climbed higher,

Then Anna saw him, an ancient musician playing the bagpipes with all his heart.

Frightened by the strange sound, Anna hid.

The piper turned, looked straight at Anna, and he smiled.

His ancient eyes sparkled as he played a bright, happy tune.

As the sun set, he played a long, sad song that echoed across the valley.

When the moon rose, he stopped. Anna listened
to the silence until the crickets began to sing.

Anna turned in the moonlight to wave good-bye
to the bagpiper. But he was gone.

When Anna told her mother all about the bagpiper,
she just smiled and shook her head.

Drifting off to sleep, Anna wondered if the bagpiper had been a dream, but then she thought she heard a faint, faraway sound.

And she did.

To Samantha

Philomel Books, a division of The Putnam & Grosset Group,
200 Madison Avenue, New York, NY 10016.
Published simultaneously in Canada.
Printed in Hong Kong by South China Printing Co. (1988) Ltd.
Book design by Nanette Stevenson.
Lettering by David Gatti. The text is set in Sabon.

Library of Congress Cataloging-in-Publication Data
Locker, Thomas, 1937–   The bagpiper/Thomas Locker.   p.   cm.
Summary: A young girl hears the strange but beautiful music of a bagpiper and
wonders if it was just a dream. [1. Bagpipers—Fiction.   2. Music—Fiction.]
I. Title.   PZ7.L7945Bag 1994   [E]—dc20   92-42350 CIP AC
ISBN 0-399-22546-3   10   9   8   7   6   5   4   3   2   1   First Impression